Copyright © 2019 by Clay Rice

Published by Familius LLC, www.familius.com

Familius books are available at special discounts for bulk purchases, whether for sales
promotions or for family or corporate use. For more information, contact Familius Sales
at 559-876-2170 or email orders@familius.com.

Library of Congress Cataloging-in-Publication Data
2019936503

Print ISBN 9781641701440
Ebook ISBN 9781641702072

Printed in China

Edited by Brooke Jorden
Cover and book design by David Miles and Derek George

10 9 8 7 6 5 4 3 2 1

First Edition

At the
Stroke
of
Goodnight

by Clay
Rice

FAMILIUS

A dreaming dog.

A purring cat.

A bird on a limb.

A mouse on a mat.

The evening glows in the twilight.
And all is quiet at the stroke of goodnight.

A creak on the stair.

A drip in the sink.

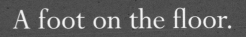

A foot on the floor.

A glass with a clink.

Everything's still and everything's right.

And all is quiet at the stroke of goodnight.

A crooning raccoon.

A squirrel on the lawn.

The faint rustle of leaves
from the doe and her fawn.

A little bear cub bathes in moonlight.
And all is quiet at the stroke of goodnight.

A calf in the barn.

A sheep in her stall.

A colt casts a shadow on the weathered wall.

A hen warms
her eggs.

Rooster waits for first light.

And all is quiet at the
stroke of goodnight.

But where is baby?

With the colt   or the cow?

With the fawn   or the sow?

On the tractor with a plow?

There she is!

A baby coos.

A mommy sighs.

Little one tucked in with dreams in her eyes,

A gentle hand turns out the light.

And all is quiet at the stroke of goodnight.